for Ollie,
with love, Giles

for Suzi Wright
with love, Emma

ORCHARD BOOKS

First published in Great Britain in 2016
by The Watts Publishing Group

1 3 5 7 9 10 8 6 4 2

Text © Giles Andreae 2016
Illustrations © Emma Dodd 2016

The moral rights of the author and illustrator have been asserted.

A CIP catalogue record for this book is available from the British Library.

ISBN 978 1 40833 962 6

Printed and bound in China

Orchard Books
An imprint of Hachette Children's Group
Part of The Watts Publishing Group Limited
Carmelite House, 50 Victoria Embankment, London EC4Y 0DZ

An Hachette UK Company
www.hachette.co.uk
www.hachettechildrens.co.uk

I love my birthday

Giles Andreae & Emma Dodd

ORCHARD

It's my birthday!

Lucky me!

I'm one year older now, you see.

Birthday kisses from my mummy.

Birthday breakfast – oh, how yummy!

We mark my height against the door.
I'm so much taller
than before.

I'm feeling more grown-up as well.

My daddy jokes that he can tell.

Look at all my presents. Wow!

Can I open this one now?

Mummy's baked
the coolest cake,
Which all my family
helped to make.

We stuck on loads
of naughty treats,
Like chocolate flakes
and button sweets!

It's time to go and play outside.

I love my brilliant birthday slide!

Now that all my friends have come

We're going to have some birthday fun!

Listen to what Daddy's saying,
"Time for party games and playing!"

Mummy starts
the birthday song,
And everybody
sings along.

See my birthday
candles glow.
I'll blow them out
in just one go!

Yum, my cake!
It tastes so nice.
I think I'll have
another slice.

Then everybody says goodbye

And Mummy gives a little sigh.

She asks if I enjoyed my day.

"I loved it, Mummy, thanks," I say.

"Well, I love you,"

she says to me.

"Now, jarmies on!

Quick, 1-2-3!"

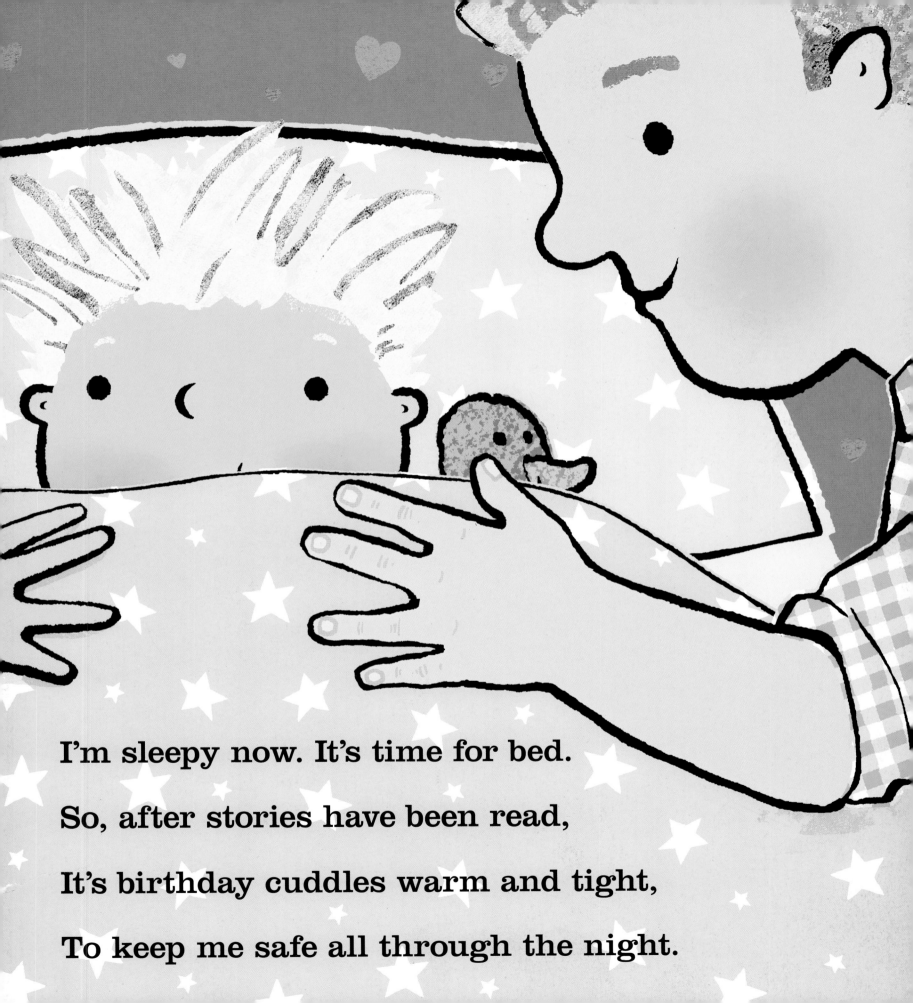

I'm sleepy now. It's time for bed.

So, after stories have been read,

It's birthday cuddles warm and tight,

To keep me safe all through the night.